MW00977377

DISNEP

THE
LION KING

HAKUNA MATATA

For Dancing Baby Jude, who, like his father, is already
teaching me the finer points of *hakuna matata*

—B. R.

To my family and my animals,
always a source of inspiration

—T. L.

Printed in the United States of America
First Hardcover Edition, June 2019

1 3 5 7 9 10 8 6 4 2
ISBN 978-1-368-03927-7
Library of Congress Control Number: 2018965045
FAC-034274-19109

Designed by Gegham Vardanyan

For more Disney Press fun, visit
www.disneybooks.com

DISNEY

THE LION KING

HAKUNA MATATA

Written by BRITTANY RUBIANO

Illustrated by THERESE LARSSON

DISNEY PRESS

LOS ANGELES • NEW YORK

Once there was a little lion cub named **SIMBA**.

Simba was staying with his pals **TIMON** and **PUMBAA** at their colorful jungle pad.

Timon and Pumbaa taught Simba how to live like them, which was turning out to be pretty great.

For one, there were **NO RULES!**

He could play with new friends and have snacks whenever he wanted (even if they mostly ate bugs). Best of all, he didn't have to take baths!

Simba was learning a lot: Like the fact
that Timon loved eggs, though they
were hard to come by.

And that Pumbaa enjoyed **BUZZARD BOWLING**.

And **HEDGEHOG BOWLING**.

And **ROCK BOWLING**.
(Really, he just loved knocking things down. Who doesn't?)

But the best thing Timon
and Pumbaa taught Simba
was their motto for an easy life:

HAKUNA MATATA.
Which means, DON'T WORRY!

The past got you down? **HAKUNA MATATA!**
Change your future.

Your favorite watering hole suddenly taken?
HAKUNA MATATA! Find a better one.

Anteaters being snooty? Be you! HAKUNA MATATA.

One morning, Simba woke up with the sun, ready to **POUNCE** on the day.

But it seemed Timon and Pumbaa were sleeping in.

Feeling antsy (and ready to hunt for grubs),
Simba decided to go exploring without them.

Soon he found a nice open field
where he could run around.

HAKUNA MATATA,

he thought happily.

A little while later, Timon and Pumbaa finally awoke
to find their friend missing.

They decided to look for Simba in all his favorite spots.

"FUR BALL!" "LITTLE BUDDY!" "SIMBA!"

They called to no answer.

"Well, this isn't good," Timon observed.

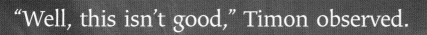

Pumbaa added, concerned.

A few clearings away, Simba was living

HAKUNA MATATA to his heart's content.

He wasn't sure how the morning
could get any better . . .

. . . until he found a perfect
MUDHOLE.

Meanwhile, Timon and Pumbaa asked their friends
if they'd seen Simba.

BUT NO ONE HAD.

They trekked farther, and soon they found a grassy field they were sure the cub would love. But he wasn't there, either.

Well, there was no denying it:

"SOMETHING TERRIBLE MUST HAVE HAPPENED!"

Timon cried. Pumbaa gasped in horror.

They were officially PANICKING.

Simba, on the other hand, was trotting cheerfully along.
He spotted some abandoned eggs high in a tree.

TIMON WOULD LOVE THOSE! he thought.

As he got closer, he noticed a few fallen logs. If those were in a pile, they'd be great for PUMBAA'S LOG BOWLING! Not to mention, they were probably crawling with bugs.

Simba grinned. He'd found the perfect gifts for his friends.

Carefully avoiding the spray of the waterfall,
he began to climb the tree.

But his little claws wouldn't hold him.

Not too far away, Timon and Pumbaa feared the worst.

"What if he fell out of a tree?"

"What if he fell into a river?"

"WHAT IF HE FELL IN WITH
THE WRONG CROWD?"

Back at the tree, Simba
tried to jump up to the
egg-bearing branch.
But yet again, his claws
slid down the trunk.

A pair of vultures
laughed at him.

"HAKUNA MATATA." Simba decided to skip the eggs.

He moved on to the logs, trying to push them into a perfect bowling pile with his snout. But they were too heavy! Hmmm . . .

Meanwhile, Timon and Pumbaa were not doing well.

"What if he was cub-napped by a giant bird?"

"What if he choked on a butterfly?"

"What if he was eaten?"

"WHAT IF HE ATE SOMEBODY?"

Just then, Simba spotted a bug on one of the logs.
He crouched, getting ready to pounce. . . .

Suddenly, he had **A BRILLIANT IDEA!**

Getting a running start, Simba sprang powerfully off the biggest log, pushing them all together. He flew into the air, through the waterfall, and toward the eggs.

"HAKUUUUNAAAA MATAAAATAAA!"

At that moment, Timon and Pumba stumbled upon the scene.

Timon and Pumbaa wailed.

"GAHHHHH! NOOOOO!
IT'S WORSE THAN WE THOUGHT!"

Simba landed and gently handed over the nest. "Guys!" he said. "I'm glad you're here! I got some eggs for you, Timon. And Pumbaa, some bowling with a side of bugs."

Timon and Pumbaa had never felt so many feelings. They were even speechless for a moment—but only for a moment.

"YOU'RE SAFE," Pumbaa finally said.

Timon choked back a sob. "And you got us presents."

Simba stared at them. "What? Were you worried?"

Pumbaa coughed. "Us? Worried? Of course not!"

"Don't be ridiculous," Timon scoffed unconvincingly.

But Simba knew exactly what his pals needed to hear right then.
"Hey, it's all right," he said with a wave of his paw.

"HAKUNA MATATA!"